WINDY WEBLEY

WINDY WEBLEY

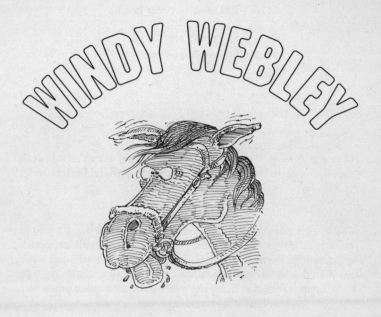

K.M Peyton

Illustrated by
Nick Price

WINDY WEBLEY
A CORGI PUPS BOOK : 0 552 545538

First publication in Great Britain

PRINTING HISTORY
Corgi Pups edition published 1997

5 7 9 10 8 6 4

Set in Bembo Schoolbook

Corgi Pups Books are published by Transworld Publishers,
61–63 Uxbridge Road, Ealing, London W5 5SA,
a division of The Random House Group Ltd,
in Australia by Random House Australia (Pty) Ltd,
20 Alfred Street, Milsons Point, Sydney, NSW 2061, Australia,
in New Zealand by Random House New Zealand Ltd,
18 Poland Road, Glenfield, Auckland 10, New Zealand
and in South Africa by Random House (Pty) Ltd,
Endulini, 5a Jubilee Road, Parktown 2193, South Africa.

Printed and bound in Great Britain by
Cox & Wyman Ltd, Reading, Berkshire.

CONTENTS

Series Reading Consultant: Prue Goodwin
Reading and Language Information Centre,
University of Reading

Chapter One

Webley was a fine black horse,
born in Ireland. When he was
full-grown, a dealer came to see
him.

"Just right for the army," he
said. "Right size, right colour,
right shape."

The army!

Begorrah! thought Webley.

He didn't want to join the army. Horses in the army were used for ceremonies, guarding the Queen, going on parade, trotting past Buckingham Palace four

by four. Army horses had to do
what they were told. They didn't
gallop or buck or bolt or fidget.
Webley liked to do all those
things.

He was given to a soldier called
Fred.

"My, you're a fine one," said
Fred. "You behave yourself and
you'll have a good life here."

Webley tried. But it was so
terribly boring.

Sometimes he had to stand still,
being a sentry in Whitehall, for a

whole hour. Fred sat on his back, bolt upright, eyes front. On the wide pavement, tourists stood and stared and took photographs.

Sometimes a tourist would stand next to Webley while his

wife took his photograph with Webley and Fred beside him. The tourist would smile and Fred would look blank. But Webley would cross his eyes, drop his ears out sideways and hang his tongue out.

Back in Japan, his photo would be shown and everyone would shriek with laughter, and the tourist would be rather cross.

"You're a right joker, you are,"
Fred said.

When Webley had done all the
things he could think of and was
really bored, he would lift his tail
slightly and make a rude noise.
This was when there was a lull in
the traffic and it was quiet.

It had an interesting effect.
Little children loved it and
laughed. But their mothers
would pretend they hadn't heard.
Fred would give him a painful
jab with his spur.

Webley found this passed the

time bearably. Sometimes he
made a quiet rude noise, and
sometimes quite a loud one.

"It's not funny, Webley," Fred
said when they were back in the
stable. "It's not good manners.
Not in public." He sighed.
"Perhaps you're not cut out for

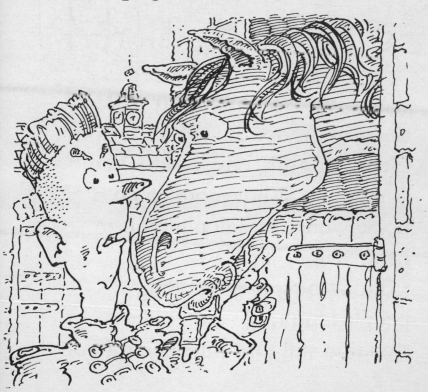

the army. You mark my words,
the army is good news for a horse.
Plenty of grub, easy work, nice
company. What more could a
horse want? It will pay you to
behave yourself."

But Webley liked making
people laugh. He didn't like
standing still for hours being good.

Chapter Two

One day there was a very
important parade. A foreign king
was visiting, with his daughter.
All the horses were drawn up on
the parade ground to await their
arrival. But the King's aeroplane
was held up and he was an hour
and a half late. The band played

and the horses got very bored and
went to sleep standing up.

At last the smart black car arrived
from the airport, and the King and
his daughter got out. The horses
all woke up and the Colonel
saluted and the band stopped
playing.

The King had to inspect the
troops – his usual job. The young

princess walked beside him, very prim. Webley could see she was as bored as he was.

The King walked slowly along with the Colonel. They were smiling. The horses mouthed their bits and pricked their ears. All except Webley, who crossed his eyes, flattened his ears and hung his tongue out.

Just as the King came past, Webley made a rude noise. It trumpeted into the stillness and echoed off the surrounding buildings.

The Colonel went red. The King smiled and walked on, but the Princess got the giggles. She tried to control them, being a well-trained princess, but she couldn't. She nearly burst. Tears came into her eyes and her chest heaved. She made a choking noise. She got

out her handkerchief and stuffed
it into her mouth, but the
choking noise burst through.
The tears spurted out of her eyes.
She went very red and tried to
pretend she had a cough.

The band started to play and

the soldiers had to ride off. The
King stood on the platform and
saluted, but behind him the
Princess nearly rolled off her chair,
choking with laughter.

At least I've cheered up her day,
thought Webley. It didn't look

much fun being a princess. He
walked along, pleased and
smiling.

But the Colonel was a sort of
purple colour with rage. When

the parade was
over, he
stormed into
the stables and
shouted at
Fred, "That
horse must go!
He does it on
purpose! He
makes fools of
us all!"

Fred knew
better than to
argue. He
thought
Webley did it
on purpose
too.

"You silly old fool," he said.
"You've gone and done it now."
Webley was sent away to the
sale-ring, and Fred shed a private
tear for he was fond of Webley.
He got a new horse called
Buster, who was very dull and
didn't mind standing still for
hours.

Chapter Three

As Webley was so handsome, he did well at the sales and was bought by a smart lady who rather fancied herself. She was called Mrs Angelina Porter-Pooter-Brown. She had black hair to match Webley, and liked

to make her cheeks very pink and
her lips very red. She wore false
eyelashes. She put on a black
jacket and a top-hat and rode
Webley in Horse Shows, which he
quite enjoyed. There wasn't as
much standing still as in the army,
and quite a bit of showing-off to do.

Mrs Angelina Porter-Pooter-Brown lived in a very big house in a smart village and was very rich. Her husband, Mr Peter Porter-Pooter-Brown, made a lot of money in the city and Mrs Angelina Porter-Pooter-Brown gave it away to good causes.

She raised money for the church. She got the village pond restored and provided seats on the village green for the elderly. The teenagers threw the seats into the village pond, but she replaced them. She had them bolted down into concrete. For all this she was much respected. But she

was very bossy and she expected
to get her own way.

In the summer the village held
a fete on the village green. Four
hundred years ago Queen
Elizabeth the First was said to
have stayed in the village and it
was decided to celebrate the visit

with a pageant. Everyone would
dress up in Tudor clothes and eat
Tudor food, and Queen
Elizabeth would arrive on
horseback with her courtiers.

Everyone would bow and a
Tudor band would play. There
would be a lot of horseplay and
drinking and some boys would
be put in the stocks for people to
throw tomatoes at. Everyone

decided which bit they would do
best. Throwing tomatoes was the
most popular, of course.

There was only one choice for
Queen Elizabeth – the only
person who actually had a horse
to ride on: Mrs Angelina Porter-
Pooter-Brown on Webley!

A lot of rehearsals took place.

Webley had to walk to the right
spot and stand still while the
Morris dancers danced, the
archers shot and the Tudor band
played. The Mayor and
Mayoress were to sit on a
platform with the vicar and the
Bigwig of the County. And

Queen Elizabeth was to deliver a long speech to the Crown about the glory of England.

When the day came, the sun shone, the crowds arrived and the tomatoes flew. The Mayor, his wife, and the Bigwig drove up in a big car and sat on the platform. The courtiers marched out and behind them came Webley, carrying Queen Elizabeth.

Webley was decked out in an old satin quilt with tassels and braided reins with fringes. Mrs Porter-Pooter-Brown wore a red wig and a white frilly ruff. So much jewellery jangled over her amazing dress that Webley felt his knees buckling. She rode Webley across the green to the platform and

pulled him to a halt.

She had a long speech to read
from a piece of rolled-up
parchment. Webley sighed and
his eyelids drooped. The speech
went on and on and, when
Webley opened one eye, he saw

the Lady Mayoress trying to stifle
a yawn. The Bigwig's head fell
forward as he dozed. It reminded
Webley of old times.

Queen Elizabeth, coming to the
end of her parchment, decried,

"What is this stirring sound? The sound of England's triumphant —" Webley made a rude noise. It started softly and rose to a

crescendo like the trumpets of the Tudor band.

Mrs Porter-Pooter-Brown's voice faltered.

Webley sighed happily.

The crowd laughed. They laughed so hard that the rest of the speech was quite drowned out.

The Bigwig woke up, wondering
what he had missed, and joined
in the general appreciation.
Everyone clapped and cheered
and shouted, and some voices
cried out, "Good old Webley!"

Webley thought he had cheered the day up no end but, when he got home, he found he was in disgrace.

Up for sale again!

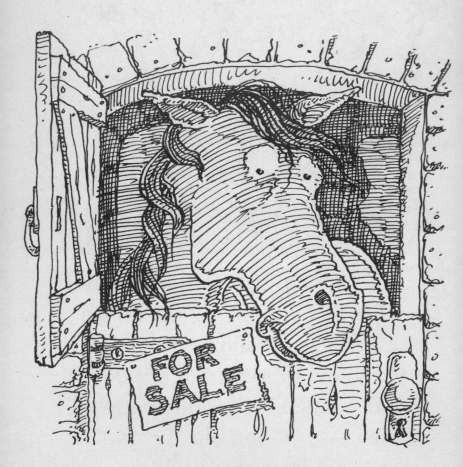

Chapter Four

This time Webley was bought by
a riding school. The work was
really boring, but when Webley
made rude noises nobody took
any notice. Webley was
disappointed and tried to think of
something else to enliven his dull
days.

They went for rides on the local
common and Webley, because he
was tall and good-looking, was
usually ridden by men who liked
to think they were smart. They
liked being up there on Webley.
Webley worked out some jokes,
like stopping suddenly and

putting his head down. If they
were holding the reins too tightly,
they shot forward down his neck.
Then Webley would shoot his
head up to 'save' them, hitting
them sharply on the nose. He
found that quite amusing. The
riding-school mistress rode him
and, when he did it, she crashed

him between the ears with her
crop so that his eyes crossed
without his meaning them to.
He didn't do it again.

Then he discovered that if he
walked under trees with the right
sort of branches the men's hats
would get caught up and they

would ride along with acorns or cherry-blossom dancing from the button on top. This looked very silly, but they didn't know until they got home.

Improving on this, he found that a quick duck under the right branch would have very

interesting results. The branch
would catch his rider across the
middle and push him out of the
saddle. Webley would take
another step and stop when the
man was sitting just on top of his
tail. He would look round as if in
surprise and the man would feel

very silly, sitting in the wrong place. If Webley didn't like him, he would walk on and leave him hanging there. Then he would lift his tail and blow him a raspberry.

Most of Webley's riders got hung on trees like this and, in the end, nobody would ride him.

"You're useless to me, Webley,"
the riding-school mistress said. "I
shall have to sell you."

She sold Webley to a girl who
wanted to go show-jumping. Her
parents bought him for her for her
birthday.

50

Webley liked sailing over the
jumps. Everyone clapped when
he jumped well. The clapping
went to his head and – for a bit
of extra show – he would give a
big buck and let out a great rude
noise after he had cleared each

jump. Everyone loved this and
clapped even harder. But, sadly
for Webley, his new rider hadn't
any sense of humour and didn't
like it. She thought he was
making a fool of her.

"You're just a clown," she told
him severely.

Webley crossed his eyes, waggled his ears and put out his tongue. He only wanted to please.

But the show-jumping girl didn't understand. She put Webley out to grass and took up tennis.

Webley was very miffed. He'd
done what she wanted, hadn't he?

Webley was out in a big field
with nothing to do and, for a bit,
he was quite happy. But when
winter came and nobody came to
look after him, he got rather
miserable. The girl's parents
decided they must sell him.

And so Webley went to yet
another home. But somehow,
everywhere he went, he kept on
getting into trouble...

Chapter Five

Finally, Webley found himself tied to a rail in a noisy market, amongst a lot of cows and sheep and some young cart-horses. He was now quite an old horse. He was also rather thin and scruffy and nothing like the smart horse he had been in his army days.

He was a bit worried as to who might buy him this time. It was well known that horses who didn't behave went down in the world. Had he been that bad? It had all been just a bit of fun really.

When his sale number was

coming near, Webley began to
feel nervous. People were looking
at him, making remarks.

"Fine horse. I wonder why he's
being got rid of?"

"Must be something wrong with
him."

Webley wanted to say, "There's nothing wrong with me!"

But they shook their heads and passed on.

Suddenly Webley saw a face he recognized, walking along and

looking at the horses. It was Fred!
Not in uniform any more, but still
looking polished and fit. He
looked straight at Webley and did
not recognize him!

Webley was desperate. What
could he do?

Of course!

He lifted his tail and blew a rude
noise.

Fred blinked, and looked again.
Webley whinnied.

"Why! I do believe – no, it can't
be! Webley? My old windy
Webley?"

Fred's voice trembled as he put
out his hand to stroke Webley's
nose. "My poor old son, what are
you doing in a rough old market
like this?"

He stood stroking Webley's dusty neck and talking to him, like old times. "I've done my time in the army, Webley, and saved up my money. I've got a nice little farm now. I've come to

buy a few sheep, but I reckon I'll
buy you instead, Webley. You and
I can work together, like we used
to."

So Webley went into the sale-
ring. And the people who thought
there must be something wrong
with him made their bids, but not

very high. When they stopped
bidding, Fred put up his hand and
Webley was sold to Fred.

Webley could not believe his
luck!

Fred took him home and put
him in a lovely stable with deep
straw and lots to eat. His wife

came out to look at Webley and his children stroked him. Webley vowed he would never do another wrong thing in his whole life.

But he might make a rude noise sometimes...

THE END